Dearest Genevees.

May God watch
over you & bless you,
and always keep you in
his loving care!

We love you,
Grandpa & NaNa
1-22-06

> Praise be to the Lord,
> to God our Savior,
> who daily bears our burdens.
> —Psalm 68:19

To the children and staff of Piddle Valley First School

With special thanks to Noah for Little Bear's drawings. —T. W.

SIMON & SCHUSTER BOOKS FOR YOUNG READERS
An imprint of Simon & Schuster Children's
Publishing Division
1230 Avenue of the Americas,
New York, New York 10020
Illustrations copyright © 2006 by Tim Warnes
Scripture quotations taken from the
Holy Bible, New International Version.
Copyright © 1973, 1978, 1984, by
International Bible Society. Used by permission.
All rights reserved, including the right of
reproduction in whole or in part in any form.
SIMON & SCHUSTER BOOKS FOR YOUNG READERS
is a trademark of Simon & Schuster, Inc.
Book design by Jessica Sonkin
The text for this book is set in Venetian.

The illustrations for this book are rendered in acrylic,
water soluble crayons, and ink.
Musical score prepared and edited by Dan Sovak.
Manufactured in China
10 9 8 7 6 5 4 3 2 1
Library of Congress Cataloging-in-Publication Data
Warnes, Tim.
Jesus loves me! / illustrated by Tim Warnes.— 1st ed.
p. cm.
ISBN-13: 978-1-4169-0065-8
ISBN-10: 1-4169-0065-9 (hardcover)
1. God—Love—Juvenile literature. 2. Jesus Christ—Juvenile
literature. 3. Hymns, English—Juvenile literature. I. Title.
BV353.W37 2005
242'.62—dc22
2005007316

Jesus Loves Me!

ILLUSTRATED BY *Tim Warnes*

Simon & Schuster Books for Young Readers
New York   London   Toronto   Sydney

Jesus loves me!
This I know,
for the Bible
tells me so.

Little ones to Him belong;

they are weak,
but He is strong.

Jesus loves me!
This I know,

as He loved so long ago.

Bear with
each other
and
FORGIVE

Taking children on His knee,

saying, "Let them come to Me."

Jesus loves me still today,

walking with me on my way.

Wanting as a
friend to give

light and love to all who live.

Yes, Jesus loves me!

Yes, Jesus loves me!

Yes, Jesus loves me!

The Bible tells me so.